FAREWELL
SOPHOMORE

ROSEMARY ARGENTE

Editor: Chris Wallace and Salma Khan

Cover: Barry McDonald
Publishers: Asaina Books
Website: asainabooks.co.uk
Email: rosa@asainabooks.co.uk

Books by the same author:

Blantyre and Yawo Women
The Veil
Praying Mantis
Difference
Share the Ride
Home From Home
Broken Temple
Essays and Poetry

Novels:
The Promised Land – Companion to The Veil
All Mine to Have
Farewell Sophomore
The Place Beyond
The Stream of Memory
A British Throne Scandal

Science Fiction:
Farewell to the Aeroplane

Booklets:
Caesar and Mapanga Homestead
Journey of Discovery
Enduring Fountain – Health and Well-being
Katherine of the Wheel
Cooking With Asaina

ACKNOWLEDGEMENTS

I am profoundly indebted to the men and women, transcending various cultures on sexuality, who have intimated to me their personal experiences. I also extend my sincere thanks to medical doctors who professionally and kindly answered my questions; and to many other persons too numerous to mention. My thanks are due to Chris Wallace and Salma Khan for editing the manuscript; to Brian Sherman, and Mark Sherman for their invaluable help; and to Barry McDonald for designing the cover. I have taken much information from Bibliography on specific heads.

For men, women, and progeny

CONTENTS

PROLOGUE 1

CHAPTER 1...3

CHAPTER 2...11

CHAPTER 3...18

CHAPTER 4...27

CHAPTER 5...39

CHAPTER 6...48

CHAPTER 7...60

PROLOGUE

The most powerful force in our existence on planet Earth is *Evolution,* or change over time, if you like, which is a *duality* process. The first has been created by the human male: explorers, inventors, architects, builders, warriors, foresters, miners, crude oil extractors, and numerous others, most of whom can be grouped as "the 'rapists' of Mother Nature" and who have surpassed all other species in changing the surface of planet Earth. In tandem with *Evolution* is *Father Time,* the Master who is blind to man's volition, and who alters everything including the human body, from conception and beyond death. If you do not accept this concept of the *duality* process of our existence then close this book, for the purpose here is to celebrate and pay tribute to all modes of *sexuality* that do no harm to anyone.

Despite that the English language is among the most expressive of languages, sadly it had been limited in other fields by the shackles of society; a regime beset with Victorian 'classes and distinctions' of morality, where sex was proper only within marriage between male and female. The oddity of the English language is that though many words have multiple synonyms for many things one of the most ubiquitous aspects of human existence has no synonym. In Latin, French and German each of the classes, typically masculine, feminine, common, or neuter of nouns and pronouns are distinguished by the different inflections attached to words syntactically associated with them.

While the mode of sexual conduct is largely influenced by the culture one has been exposed to as set by man, there had been no proper label for other sexual unions other than within heterosexual marriage. This glaring omission is partly due to the lack of open societal acknowledgement of other forms of union, though they may be in a relationship that is more loving, faithful, and lasting than a good number of the so-called 'legal marriages' in which the divorce rate figures speak for themselves. 'Partner' is a label that developed in both heterosexual and homosexual unions though one that took hold in recent years. All went along with girlfriend, boyfriend, but the universal connotation of these obsolete words sits uncomfortably with those of a certain age. The more mature-sounding 'man friend' and 'woman friend' are clumsy and imprecise. The French *'paramour'* (literally 'for love') is unfortunately unsuitable because its connotation is of illicit affair. Equally the French *'beau',* is exclusively for a boyfriend or male admirer. 'Mistress' implies a kept woman, despite that she may have resources in her own right and probably supporting the man; and whatever label she and her man may choose to use, "Constant Companion" or whatever, society will apply its own 'legal' stamp of 'mistress'. The term 'Suitor' is too stiff, does not imply an everlasting union, and applies only to the male. 'Life partner' would seem to imply some bureaucratic policy; 'domestic partner' has the disadvantage of assuming cohabitation. And many other terms are unsuitable as they fail to express the nature of the relationship. So, it was left to introduction only by name and let non-verbal signals do the rest.

CHAPTER 1

COLIN WAS LEANING against the railway platform pillar as if to support his broken form, bereft at the thought of never seeing her again.

"Please, please, don't leave", he pleaded.
Amrita had implored him not to come to the railway station but he nurtured the hope that he could persuade her to change her mind.

****

AMRITA FOUND THE STREET she was looking for in Springfield, a short street with a long name, "Longfield." There was a place to park her blue Honda on the right side of Longfield. She ascended the few steps to number "One Thousand", yet again, a high number for a short street. She rang the front door bell. A red head with a winning smile answered the door.

"I'm registered with Vienna College and the vocational course in interior designing. I believe I will be staying here", Amrita said.

"You must be our Room Two mate". The red head replied.

"How is that?"

"The other four took up their rooms in the last two days. The only one to be taken up is Room Two", Kathleen explained, in a typical "little-mother-of-the house" fashion, while assisting Amrita with her baggage into the spacious Edwardian style hall.

Kathleen, short and frumpy, was a very attractive Irish Colleen, her flaming tresses cascaded beyond the rear groove of her waistline. Since the early nineties, long hair had again become trendy, resembling the tresses of the Edwardian women, if One Thousand was to tell its own story. Kathleen had done well at the age of twenty-two. She explained that she was registered at Dublin College.

"I'm doing a Master's in public health and I also attend at Ninewells Hospital."
They stood in the hall. Amrita noticed, unfamiliar to her, the heat storer affixed to one side of the wall at the same time observing the high ornate ceilings of the house and remarked: "Isn't it rather warm and welcoming in here?"
"You should see your room. It's the best in the house."

Kathleen took the key from Amrita, holding one piece of baggage with the other hand, she led the way to the first floor. They ascended the ornate carved staircase holding to its black shiny banisters. Amrita observed the ingenuity of the house locks; every single key of each of the five rooms opened the front door and yet each key was exclusive to its individual door. How do they manage that? She wondered.

Kathleen proceeded on the introductory layout of the house. On the top floor, what once had obviously been a huge attic was the main bathroom/toilet en suite adjacent to a beautifully converted bed sit. The occupier of this, she was told, was Katia who chose Leningrad College to complete her Master's in petroleum law. Evidence of the caring touch abounded around the various public areas in the interior of the house. Neat little notices with minute drawings of human faces and daisies and in non-aggressive language were apparent appeals for hygiene and tidiness to which Kathleen confessed herself to be the artist.

On the ground floor and into the sitting/dining area, Amrita could hear voices. Kathleen points out the downstairs bathroom at the far rear end of the house. Through the only other door leading out is a bare bleak garden, as most European gardens in the autumn. Amrita was pleased at the huge tall silver birches and shrubs in the garden of the adjacent house.

"Where there are trees and leaf there is bound to be bird song", she remarked.

The two houses are separated by a hedge sparsely in complement to the complex covered in dried up in leaves is a charred-looking honeysuckle.

They enter the dining/kitchen area where the voices had come from and where four inmates were sat around a table with a white Formica top.

"At last we are all assembled together", says the little mother as she made the introductions.

Harriet was in her final year of her horticultural course at Rome College. Robust, bubbling with life, the outdoor girl announced that on the morrow she was to continue her swimming recreation. She is wearing no make-up and her light brown hair was cut in a short, boyish style. She was rather mature for her twenty-two years and attractive in a plain sort of way. Almost always, she was clad in that hard-wearing unisex informal garment associated with cowboy heroes; preferred by most modern women for its dual value, easy to maintain and its sexy tight fit, successor to the model without the front zipped flies (flies prescribed illegal for the women of pre-sixties) had made the pioneering astute Mr Levi Strauss a multi millionaire.

Bibi enjoyed a dual culture, though on her first arrival in Scotland she felt somewhat isolated. She came from Mozambique and had enrolled at Lisbon College. She had joined her English husband on his two-year tour as a lecturer in architecture at the University of Edinburgh. They had been married for twenty-five years and had a grown up son and daughter.

Born in St Petersburg, the city that changed its name to Leningrad under Lenin and back to its original name at the end of the Cold War, Katia was very much a woman of the world for her twenty-four years. She carried her head high on well balanced shoulders and was the proud owner of a million dollar pair of legs. Her hazel eyes were hard and as icy as the Cold War. Rather feminine in her mode of dress and countenance she was no contributor to Levi's coffers.

"How do you like Britain, or rather Scotland I should say?" Amrita ventures to ask Katia.

"It's alright, but very different. When you go out the men don't pay. Not like that in Russia."

Katia made no bones about her priorities in pecuniary punctilio. The absence at the assemblage of the usual never ending topic of the "battle of the sexes", left Amrita wondering as to whether her fellow residents may not all be heterosexual.

"We are all going to see *Forest Gump*, featuring Tom Hanks (playing the character that may have made Hanks an actor). Would you like to come?" Says the little mother.

"I think I should unpack. Thanks anyway."

****

AMRITA SURVEYED HER NEW ABODE. It was spacious and amply furnished, a writing desk and lots of fitted shelves gave her plenty of room for her numerous books and bundles of drawings on properties she had prepared over the years. The spacious massive room was reduced by a wall and an archway which gave the effect of two rooms. There was no question of getting out of the wrong side of the bed, for it was located against the far end wall. The pride features of the room were two tall large Edwardian windows, adorned by lace curtains over which were full length curtains of a floral design fabric on a background of emerald green echoing the upholstery of the odd armchair. She adjusted the chair and placed it where she could see Perth Road below through the lace curtains. She sat in it, sipping a cup of nettle tea and observed the passing parade below, without being seen – spying as it were (more appropriately 'espying').

A particular place at a given time cuts a picture of a specific scene of the setting sun peering through a cluster of buildings flanking Perth Road. The road runs almost parallel to the tidal River Tay, a river large enough to swallow Father Thames twenty times over. The silhouette figures from different walks of life in the early evening dwindling light are part of the passing parade along Perth Road. All with a single purpose, "homeward bound" at the end of whatever their daily occupations. All that is comprised of the universe, natural and cultural, the curiosity of the eye, the lust of the flesh, pride of place in the universe, all would come to pass, she thought. Can anyone tell me what will last?

"Yes, the supreme knowledge of the immortal self, the soul", answering her own question.

Amrita was jolted by the sharp loud ringing of the door bell. She hurried down the stairs and opened the front door. She was looking into the amiable sky-blue eyes of a young man.

"I am supposed to be staying here. Is this Anderson House?

"I doubt that you could be staying here. This is an exclusively female accommodation."

"Oh! I'm in the wrong place, then."

"You'll have to look for an exclusively male place. I believe there is one on the other side of this same street. Almost opposite to this house. That might be Anderson House." Amrita explained.

"My mail should be arriving here. There must have been some mistake, somewhere. Would you mind holding any mail that comes for me, please?"

"What name?"

"Colin McGregor."

"Sure. I will." Amrita ventured at conversation by asking what he was studying.

"I am a sophomore in Scots law at Edinburgh College." He replied.

"Sophomore. That's Americanism, isn't it? She went on.

"Yes. I rather like the word for a second year student." He replied.

"How was your first year?" Amrita went on.

"I have enjoyed it very much." Colin replied.

****

COLIN IS TALL AND WELL BUILT as one born and bred on a farm. His hands were soft and cared for without any trace of farm manual labour. He had never been exposed to the arena of life. He was a helper to his widowed father in sheep farming on the Isle of Bute where he lived a restricted sheltered life. Fiona, his twin sister, had naturally slipped into the role of domestic chores and was relied upon as mother of the house since their mother passed on when they were in their early teens.

From outside of his small world Colin had no mentor, aside from the reserved guidance of his father. He had been a bright child at school. At the age of sixteen he had completed his "A" levels with distinction.

Even though science does not describe the tangible world but makes an attempt to explain how the world interacts with the human mind, Colin was well informed and his general knowledge was derived from literature. His outstanding understanding of geography, for one who had never ventured beyond his island until he came to Brighouse, surprised Amrita. But then the Scots are great explorers and when they are not literally exploring, they do so through literature.

****

FOR THE LAST TWENTY YEARS Amrita had been beloved wife to Christian, ten years her senior. They had shared the privileges and responsibilities of their union, each respecting and acknowledging the capabilities of the other for their worth. They had regarded each other as a separate whole being to a union, the freedom of avoiding total fusion in rejection of the preference to the notion of 'my better half' which most married couples seem to adopt: "I am me" and "you are you" – an echo of Alex Comfort's *The Joy of Sex*.
That was another time, another place, with a bent back counting the millions in property development shared with her husband. She had much to sort out and had convinced herself that a second bite of the cherry as occupational therapy might give her a boost to ease the pain of past reflections.

Their only son, David, the image of Christian, was a lecturer in anthropology at Witwatersrand University in South Africa. Christian had moved on into the next world. It is through the loss of the self that you identify with the loss of a loved one. Every relationship takes much of oneself but nothing is permanent – we may find it easier to let go, let painful experiences be replaced by happy memories.

Her large brown eyes, alert, gave no trace of her advanced years though the dark shadows under them reflected her sadness, death maims the surviving partner, man or woman. She recalled the lines of a friend's poem the year before:

9

"There is no reality, only memory is the reality.
In the stream of memory I am only but a ripple..."

She feels and moves with the agility of a twenty-year old. Parental restrictions had influenced her failure to muster such agility at twenty. Amrita wore no make up, she was very much the nature's child, seeking to grasp and hold youth in Mother Nature herself. In most things she did she adhered to the natural, a preference for herbal treatments, herbal intakes and natural moisturisers, such as avocado and olive oil.

Of less than medium height her posture is erect, physically delicate though amply compensated by the strength of spirit. The colour of her hair, black splashed with red lights, shows no sign of silver strands as that of her paternal grand mother, who never turned grey until aged seventy-nine. She had always envied her mother's white silk tresses. Typical, if you don't have it you want it! Save for a gold Omega watch on her wrist and a single string of white beads, a gift from her mother for 'good luck', adorning her swan-like neck, Amrita had deposited all her exquisite jewellery, what Christian had lovingly lavished upon her, into a bank for personal security, setting to rest the pain of beautiful memories of their years together.

CHAPTER 2

BRIGHOUSE CAMPUS SPANS OVER a hundred-acre site on the eastern fringe of the City of Dundee near Forfarshire. Brighouse is the replica of the standard universities dotted around cities of member states, which had removed the commercial aspect whereby students were regarded as 'customers'. Students may register with any one of the colleges, named after the capital cities of member states. The degrees are awarded by the parent institution of the European Union which funds Brighouse on equal opportunity to citizens of its fifty-five member states and each student is alumnae to the college registered with.

The curriculum is comprised of two levels of study: a three-year undergraduate course and one year of vocational post-graduate as an optional complement to the former. There are no lectures or lecturers. All study material is computer based. A tutor of the course leads bi-weekly seminars and emphasis is placed on a student's full participation in seminar discussions.

The campus, inadequate to accommodate the full capacity of twenty thousand students, offers accommodation in halls of residence only to undergraduate first years. The rest of the students seek rented accommodation from various landlords. It is the time of the prime of the *mature student.*

Conservative Britain is still engaged in the never ending debate on the sovereignty of Brussels over Westminster. It is a time of diverse rights realised when the differences of age, ethnicity, religion, gender, physical disability and cultures are inconsequential. Hitherto, lifestyle had been determined by institutional ageism, a social and legal response to the aged. The absence of positive legislation against ageism had meant a voluntary approach in giving opportunities in the employment field as in the study area. But now the door was open and mature student numbers increased in universities.

The major convenor is a three-dimensional spontaneity: the same degree, the same semester and the same hour of seminars and the student's faculties absorbed knowledge in a particular chosen field. In this replica of our universe a great number of women and men are converged in make-believe-love in the indulgence of the pleasures of the flesh but also highlighting flitting relationships and some to face the inevitable consequences. It is a case of do or die, a war was on as it were. In this prodigal *rite of passage* they face a diversity of circumstances, such as unwanted pregnancies, but more particularly, the evanescence of true love.

****

AMRITA STRIVED TO ARRIVE at the seminar long before the appointed hour to choose a place close to the dais so she could have an unobstructed view of the seminar leader she had heard so much about. There are already seated three young blondes. She senses the hostility of one of the blondes. As fate would have it, Colin attends the same seminar at the same hour, walks in and sits next to Amrita.

Angus McManus, the suave seminar leader, glides into the full attendance. Before he takes his place at the dais, he proceeds to remove, first his sun glasses - Amrita wondered 'where is the sun'? - then his gloves, and black leather jacket. He removes each item in night-club strip-teaser style, relishing each gesture as if he were God's gift for women - and men?

The subject is on general principles of contract law which Amrita had added to her interior decorating course, to give her strength in dealing with contractual matters.

"This is a Christian country, and that is our culture", says one of the blonds.

"Is this seminar on Christianity?" Amrita asks.

Angus appears lost.

"I think we are embarking on dangerous ground here", says Amrita, as she realises that it was a personal attack upon her...

****

STUDENTS USUALLY MEET at the popular venue after the seminar, the Tower Café. From the top floor the view of the River Tay and surrounding area is exquisite. The commodious docks are in the confines of the River Tay throughout the stages of the tide, twelve miles from the sea. There is also a small shipyard at the eastern end of Dundee where the Tay flows towards the North Sea.

In the Café, Amrita meets Laura Guttenburg who explains that she and her husband Jim had agreed that the long spells of three weeks separation in each month was a small price to pay for Jim's lucrative job. He was an engineer in the North Sea. They had a daughter aged twenty-five from Laura's previous liaison and two sons aged eighteen and twenty. Laura enjoyed what Jim lavished upon her and she spoke of Jim, their house, possessions, and their three offspring as if she was blissfully happy. Situated in the select area of Broughty Ferry their home was ordinary and over tidy, as Amrita noted at Laura's invitation. At the one end of the cum sitting dining area was the pride piece of the dining room, a highly polished imitation mahogany dining table and six chairs en suite. More appropriate for a house with a separate

13

dining room, since the table was used only on special occasions - they normally ate in the kitchen. The rooms of the entire house boasted a degree of affluence in "things", from Jim's lucrative earnings.

The furniture, furnishings and ornately framed copies of old and modern masters hang on the walls. Bookshelves were filled with quality bound books they had never read - there are none so vulnerable as consumers. Laura was a shopaholic and the walls of their house suffered eternal alterations to accommodate "things". A family typical of the saying: "from clogs, to riches, to clogs."

Broughty Ferry was once the prime of the jute industry, second to Glasgow as a manufacturing centre in the leading world of jute production and had accommodated the wealthy jute merchants. Their factory workers concentrated in the less salubrious areas of Dundee. Even in modern times middle aged women adorned in diamonds and rubies was not an unusual sight in the streets of Broughty Ferry.

The reasonable side of Jim supports Laura's pursuit of her dream and he even takes pride in her studies. After all he had agreed to move from Germany and purchase a house in Broughty Ferry to live there for three years, the duration of time for her to obtain a Forensic Science Degree. The other part of him, unwitting to either of them, is plagued by the fear of losing her. She is entering a world alien to him, even though he is a professional in his own right. Their arguments begin to escalate to stress levels, the typical archaic syndrome - a case of evolution versus stagnation. Trapped in the status quo, Jim seeks some anaesthetic to numb the pain. He indulges in excessive intake of Scotch whisky and tries to satisfy his craving for nicotine. Clearly there was a sex war here. Sex wars, like all wars endure where there are opposing ideals. Sexual wars often arise where men, particularly those over fifty, according to the view of some women, refuse to accept that they may be on the descent, a condition they choose to attribute to women. The shortcoming is two-fold: the archaic syndrome, the desire of men to maintain the status quo – there is a good number of women in this stream too – and the aspiration of women to seek a personal identity - all to the forfeiture of their own happiness.

In most cases, both men and women fail to recognise the importance of context in the ever-changing cosmos that govern our lives. For the women who accept the status quo, who do not seek a personal identity, or are morally supported by their men if they seek a personal identify, there are no sex wars.

****

LAURA HAD GIVEN JACOB, her favourite, the first refusal. Jim would be away on duty during the Summer Ball but in any event she had preferred "one of the boys" to be her escort.

"You know me, Laura, music and dancing is not my scene", Jacob had declined. He certainly was not the "dinner by candlelight" or city night lights type. Laura had paid for the hotel accommodation and for the ball tickets as well, making certain she booked two single rooms, at the total cost of £300. She could well afford it given her husband's lucrative position.

The hairdresser's skill, at some astronomical outlay, well camouflaged her silver threads. Her fashionably styled blond tresses fell beyond her well balanced broad shoulders, covering the sides of her pretty face. The severe hairstyle, smooth front and tie back which characterised the image of Evita or Eva Peron would do little for many a feminine facial feature. Laura was astute in choosing her hairstyle.

Kathleen looks gorgeous in a wine coloured sleeveless ball gown and matching accessories. The hairdresser had given her a perfect crowning glory.

"This is John".

Kathleen, holding a single red rose, introduces her escort to Amrita. He was wearing a black dinner suit and exquisite accoutrements. He is a fine young man and he is doing things in style.

****

GARY CALLS ON AMRITA, whistles:

"You look delightful." He says. He had known no manual labour or sport that are so good for the human body as one born and bred in a city.

Amrita continues to listen patiently to his overtures. Gary is playing the aggressive pursuer of his contemporary fancy. She gives no clue as to the opinion she is forming of him, the macho, in action. This gives him the courage he needs.

"I am deeply attracted to you". I have sex with Miss Body Beautiful on Tuesdays and Thursdays. I want you for Wednesdays and Saturdays."

Gary could not have been blunter. He is playing the skilful actor who vacillates between the aggressor and the victim, the confounded liar in the game to achieve success in capturing woman of the moment. He makes a symbolic show of pursuit and simulates surrender to Amrita's charm. Amrita goes to the door and opens it with her left hand and a sweeping gesture with her right indicates the way out.

"Oh!" Gary stammers, I meant no offence." Quietly but audibly she utters one word, "Out!".

In a flash he is out of Room Two. He has played one role to the exclusion of the other. Thanks to his inept approach. "Better luck with the next one," he thinks to himself as he walks towards his male abode off Perth Road on the eastern

16

side of the city. He would waste no time trying his luck with the next one. It is now well into the first quarter of the semester when one and all of the students have settled in.

CHAPTER 3

THE FERRY APPROATED THE QUAYSIDE. Amrita had changed trains at Glasgow to catch the 1:30 ferryboat for the Isle of Bute. It was a beautiful clear day in spring. She observed as she boarded the boat, how beautiful the scenery without, but sadly when she took her seat the view was obscured as the windows of the ferryboat were too high. She would have loved to observe the scenery as they sailed along.

As she walked down the disembarking plank, she gasped at the panoramic, pictorial view of the ups and downs of the terrain of the island, carpeted in different shades of green, some light grey mingling of colours like a flat hand-embroidered piece of fabric. A variety of springtime blossom lent a touch of beauty and romance. There was something very enchanting about islands, she thought. Bute reminded her of Likoma Island she had once visited in Malawi, Africa – while the islandesque charm was somewhat similar, the layout of Bute was totally different in the terrain of the land.

Bute lies in the Firth of Clyde in Scotland. It is divided into highland and lowland areas by the Highland Boundary Fault. At some point the UK press painted Bute as a place with no future. During the Viking era Bute was known as Rothesay, possibly in reference to the personal name of Roth or Roderick and the Old Norse suffix 'ey' ('island'). This name was eventually taken by the main town on the island, whose Gaelic name is Baile Bhoia (town of Bute).
Later, she also noted the placid easy going manner of the people, what would be termed as *alekific* (Arabic), was a characteristic of island people, as she had also observed in the Caribbean. Waiting at the quayside was Colin, his father

and Fiona. Colin, the only driver in the family, took the wheel of the family car, the preliminaries and introductions over. The drive was short, through the town with shops not unlike any other parts of Britain. Colin pointed out an island retreat, a homestead all in white, including the outbuildings, property of Richard Attenborough.

To all intents and purposes, Amrita was a guest in the main house. She was shown to one of the bedrooms where her light baggage was placed. In recent years she learned to travel light. Then they all settled at the father's table to a superb healthy meal of braised steak, a mixture of steamed green vegetables and mashed potatoes. She had brought a cake, the famous rich, fruit, Dundee cake, with whole almonds on top. It was most welcome as a scrumptious dessert. She observed that like most Scots she had met, not only abroad, Colin's father was a very well read man with a good general knowledge, even in that remote part of farm land of the Isle of Bute.

****

COLIN SAVOURED EVERY MOMENT OF IT. After the meal Colin took her and the farm's two black and white sheep dogs on a tour of the farm, mainly a sheep farm. They had walked through his father's livestock grazing land surrounded by the picturesque scenery of that exquisite enchanting island.

The sun was like a ball of amber in the west and the evening had almost swallowed up the dying amber splashes in the sky. It was twilight.

"Excuse me!" Amrita looked up and noticed that the dogs had ventured too far ahead of them, and had stopped abruptly, obedient to Colin's canine command. They had walked on till the evening had swallowed up all the dying amber splashes in the sky, marking the end of the day.

"It is now time to turn back", Colin announced.

"Is it a full moon?" looking up he asks.

"You tell me, Colin, it's your moon." She says.

The moon seemingly suspended in a sky turned to the hue of blue-grey, though not similar, reminded her of St Helena, the island she had once visited on her way back to Africa where Napoleon lived in the last days of his life and died in captivity.

Colin's abode is a two-bedroom guest cottage on his father's farm. He had been receiving a job seeker's allowance. Amrita had learned that there were several kinds of allowances in Britain, the welfare state. Now Colin received instead a European Union education grant to cover his study of the undergraduate degree. The walk is over, exhilarated, they have now arrived at the door of Colin's abode and they enter. Within Amrita proceeds to educate the naïve Colin.

She begins by asking him:

"Do you know the definition of a kiss?"

"No". He replies.

"The juxtaposition of two olfactory glands to produce stimulation which can be measured by an electroencephalograph."

"Sounds like a scientific definition", he remarked.

To give immediacy to the fleeting moment as the ideal she kisses him, not by the so-called French kiss, mouth to mouth where one person inserts the tongue into another's mouth, or the tongues meet (McOwen) but by moving her lower lip, and kissing the interior of his mouth. Amrita's own brand of the passion-kindling kiss - no woman ever got impregnated by just a kiss..

****

****

FOR ONE SO KNOWLEDGEABLE Amrita was surprised when their conversation had turned to the definition of love. Colin exhibited a 'naïve' kind of interest in matters of the heart and sexual love that Amrita was obliged to conclude he was a virgin at thirty-seven. His chance meeting with her was to change all that as she began to impart her own concept of the meaning of love: an all embracing quality not confined to that of man and woman but to its many facets and she asked:

"How come you have attained the age of thirty-seven without knowing the beauty of woman, as most men usually do?"

"Staunch Roman Catholicism is a very strict upbringing." He replied.

She began by giving him the definition of true love that embraces every kind of relationship:

Love is the energy of life,

> Where love is God is.
> Let me not defer it or neglect it,
> For, I shall not pass this way again...
> -Robert Browning

There are numerous faces of love: the love for a child; parent; sibling, good temper for the siblings, replica of the self, for there is no scale to balance their misdemeanour; spouse; friend; and a whole host of other relationships. Also true love is courtesy in relation to etiquette in the community, society and beyond in the relation of international communications; and what is within the universe holistically. For example, the separated or divorced couples in their squabbles are oblivious to the welfare of their children because they have lost the love plot, as the enduring basis of each of the objects of love is *friendship*.

Love is the many splendoured thing. But sadly, utter the word

'Love' and most minds will conjure up "sexual activity", a universal misunderstanding of the word. Others search for love in sexual activity but sex and love are entirely separate. Sex speaks for a fundamental human need but it is essential to distinguish between responsible sex and irresponsible sex; and sex is an art in itself independent from love or lust. Two separate conditions, as apparent in prostitution, one-night stands, group sex, orgies, and many other situations that do not involve the commitment by two persons, whether heterosexual or homosexual. Sexual love combines personal fulfilment attached to certain values: *sexuality,* the classifier; *fantasy*, erotic imagination; *sustenance*, victuals to maintain energy; *grace*, is peaceful existence; and *sexual orientation,* culture.

Sexual love is depicted by a blind metaphor symbolised by Cupid, or *Cupido* (Latin, son of Venus the goddess of love), the Roman god of love, beautiful naked, winged boy with bow and arrows. *Cupido* translated is desire, passion, lust or greed, an indication of the thin line that divides love and lust. (Perhaps this is why the Romans invented Cupid!.) From this translation one may say Cupid applies only to sexual love. Despite restrictions imposed by social and cultural differences or systems of governments, universally over the centuries, individuals have defied prescriptions and transcended barriers to mate in clover to the derision of their peers. The former South Africa's apartheid legislation hopelessly failed to stop mating among the different races. The mechanics of procreation are blind (*Cupid*?) to differences and are primordial to the perpetuation of species universally and historically. Though to procreate is not always the object of a union as apparent in homosexuality.

The individual's perception of the concept of Eros (Greek, or Cupid Latin: Some myths make him a primordial god, while in other myths, he is the son of Aphrodite. He was one of the winged love gods, *Erotes*, origin of 'erotic') is conditioned from early childhood by an established system of law and order in two-dimensional principles, under the reality and beyond the reality (Freud). This view indicates that law and society impose rules of morality upon individuals. Prior to the passing of legislation to curb anti-social behaviour, it was believed that this was a subject that could not be legislated; though it is unclear as to whether morality is a subject that could be legislated. This leaves open the question as to how far our existence is improved by the imposition of rules of morality, and whether morality applies only to matters sexual. In the twentieth-century the Western world held an immense fascination with distinctive types of erotic behaviour and re-wrote the concept of sexuality. Since the break-free ideology of the Sixties and the transparency embracing most aspects of human existence a fair exchange emerged (Argente, *Difference*).

In the Freudian concept of Eros, under the reality principle, cultural constraints affect both social and biological existence. Culture prohibits a wanton Eros and instinctual volitions are not regarded as involuntary and their manifestations must give way to the transformation from a *pleasure* principle to a *reality* principle. A transformation seen by some as man's regression from development. The reality principle is ingrained into the individual's perception from early childhood enforced by parents and other educators, which Freud calls the *archaic heritage*, and which the individual's memory traces to the experiences of previous generations (Ondaatje). Human instincts are permanently suppressed for a higher cause, that of civilisation (whatever the word means!); that happiness is not a cultural value but controlled libido reflects a cultured person. A concept which governs Western civilisation, according to Freud (Dollimore). Beyond the reality principle is the domination of man and nature to the sublimation of society and morality. Unlike the external wanton Eros, the reality principle is ordered Eros and internalised aggression. *Beyond the reality* principle reflects the pastor and prelate, which seeks a perfect destiny beyond the present at the expense of a better *here and now*; and as according to an established system of law and order. The suppression of the individual's instincts from infancy prevents development of the individual's instinctual abilities (Marcuse).

Language asserts the misnomer *fall in love* to underline the loss of balance or misconstruction of language? Fall is no merit since one falls into error, debt or disgrace. Love is confused with lust, the desire of the senses. Loneliness and the longing to be loved motivate some to seek solace only to find it in a mistaken synonym for love. The sexual act itself, whether motivated by love or lust is called "love-making". The Oxford English Dictionary (and other dictionaries) translates 'paedophilia' as "sexual love directed towards children". That such cruelty to children can be referred to as 'love' is an impertinence upon the English language. The term *straight* in the description of the heterosexual connotes other modes of sexual activity as *bent* (Argente, *Difference*).

Fact and fantasy combine in sexual love or sexual lust. Some naturally aspire to the ideal. Mind and body are central to our being. Mind combines heart, spirit and soul. Soul is generally associated with what is good, the moral aspect of the individual and is immortal, present at conception and after death as some believe, though not others but each to own opinion. Soul is generally attributed to intellectual qualities: honourable conduct: "I hope this will awaken the soul" so it is said; sometimes revealed in works of art; and the American Black Culture (political correctness to the outmoded Negro-hood) is expressed in soul music. Conduct can destroy the soul of another where actions fail to reflect inner goodness, or 'love', if you like.

The one major component that aids the many faces of love is *grace*, the bedrock of true enduring love. Grace embraces a number of values and its key elements are *kindness* towards others; *self-less* and *decorum* in conduct, *felicity* in refinement; *permission* in *acceptance*, and *splendour* and *loveliness* in human embrace; and applies to all relationships. Grace in sexual love is perfected by psychological factors: trust, openness, a combination of modesty and ostentation and a state of well-being. Grace gives energy to those we come into contact with and thereby we may receive energy in return.

For the lovers, spouses are lovers too, Amrita explained, are essentials in the duality of the combination of body and soul: The *ambience,* comfortable, peaceful, pleasing setting conducive to complete relaxation; the *surrender,* the mental preparation, the relinquishing of the ego, the banishment of guilt; inhibitions, and the giving of self permission the acceptance of *erotology,* a state of mind in fantasy; *tenderness,* mental delight that a natural joyous and harmonious act could not be wrong and the paying of homage to the lover; the *Tantra* (in Oriental sexual practice) where enjoyment of sex lies in the prolonged experience of ecstasy the interplay of the two great forces of the cosmos, Yin and Yang and orgasm is not the goal. Tantric sex is not confined to geriatrics. The tasting of the wine is irrelevant rather the lovely ardour after drinking it (Comfort). Human relationship tries to combine the two, sex and love, some with a degree of success but disastrous for others; delay the *climax,* to hold the act. The turn-offs may include anxieties, such as "must post that letter" and all sorts of other distractions which create no environment to mental preparation.

In the many varieties of ablutions, hygiene is important to most, not so to others. Napoleon on homeward bound would send an advance message to his woman to abstain from a bath. For some, smell is a turn on, as when Nico and Alkie (nicotine and alcohol) oozing out in abusive bedroom language is a turn on for some but nauseating for others. In ancient peoples, the Romans surpassed. The bath was not a mere amenity for satisfying their obsession for personal hygiene but also for relaxation and political priorities. In modern times the French, and other Continentals, excel over their Western counterparts by favouring the *bidet*, as part of their plumbing regulations. In Islam, it is imperative as a mark of reverence to Allah for a prior ablution to prostrate on a mat facing the East; where also before and after the sexual act, ablution is considered as part of the sanctity of sexual love.

****

ALL WERE AT THE BREAKFAST TABLE save the father who had his breakfast early and was away tending to the sheep. Breakfast was the usual healthy bowl of porridge oats, prepared by Fiona. After breakfast Colin offers to show Amrita the layout of his accommodation...When the opportunity presented itself she would give him the next stage, that on 'sexuality', as she had promised.

CHAPTER 4

Sexuality

SEXUALITY IS A COMBINED CONDITION of the mental and physical aspects, the classifier, and the capacity for sexual feelings. Sexuality distinguishes between to have a sex and to have sex; sex appeal; sexual orientation; a sexed body one able to perform with a relatively fixed object: preference to a particular mode of sexual performance and the major turn on is the type of partner: heterosexual, opposite sex, homosexual, same sex; bisexual, one who feels equally at home with either; and solitaire, masturbation. The traditionally accepted aim is the union of the genital organs of male and female but there are many features that alter this aspect influenced by a number of factors, such as individual preference, geriatric condition, or a fixed fantasy, and others. Sexuality is largely conditioned by culture motivated by draconian religious obsession with morality (Argente, *The Veil*), though some break through cultural norms to find their own sexual identity – indulging in their own kind for sexual liberation.

Creation is awesome. Messages on sexuality can be seen in some plants and trees. The *Peristeria elata* is a species of orchid that is found from Central America to Ecuador and Venezuela. It is the type of species of its genus and commonly referred to as the Holy Ghost orchid, dove orchid or flower of the Holy Spirit in England, and as the *flor del Espiritu Santo* in Spanish. It is white and looks like a dove when in full bloom. Before the flower fully blooms it slightly resembles a praying mantis.

Certain aspects of sexuality are also attached to trees. The most fitting example is the paw paw tree. The female paw paw tree yields well-ripened paw paw fruit, whereas the male tree produces useless lanky never maturing fruit, not unlike the non-lactating male breasts.

Perhaps the most fascinating is the palm tree of the *Coco de mer* endemic to the Seychelles islands of Praslin and Curieuse. The female plant yields large nuts like the shape and size of a woman's disembodied buttocks on one side, and a woman's belly and thighs on the other side. The male tree has long phallic-looking catkins. Both plants are of erotic shapes. One of its many legends has it that the island of Praslin was the original Biblical Garden of Eden and that the *Coco de mer* was the forbidden fruit of the tree of knowledge of good and evil (Wikipedia).

Sexual sex reveals that penetration and orgasm are not essential to joyful and satisfying sex but openness, trust, love, friendship, technique, mechanics and time; and sex very much depends upon the individual. Some have a high sex libido, others medium, low or nil for men as for women (Kinsey Reports). According to Western literature the world is conditioned to the belief that sex is culturally created.
According to oral tradition among the non-Western sex is viewed as biologically given. Sex speaks for a fundamental human need and is basic to all humans but paramount is the distinction between responsible sex and irresponsible sex (Argente, *Blantyre and Yawo Women*).

LGBT or GLBT
IS AN INITIALISM THAT STANDS FOR lesbian, gay, bisexual, and transgender. It may be used to refer to anyone who is non-heterosexual or non-cisgender (cisgender is a slightly narrower term for those who do not identify as transgender – a larger cultural category than the more clinical

transsexual) instead of exclusively to people who are lesbian, gay, bisexual or transgender. Homosexulity is sexual attraction to people of one's own sex. Lesbian is a woman whose sexual orientation is to women (Argente, *Difference*, chapter 6, Minorities, Homosexuality, for the origin of lesbian on the island of Lesbos, Greece). The word 'Gay' arrived in English during the 12th century from Old French gai, most likely deriving ultimately from a Germanic source. In English, the word's primary meaning was "joyful", "carefree", "bright and showy", and the word was very commonly used with this meaning in speech and literature (now evolved to the male homosexual). Bisexual is sexually attracted to both men and women. Transsexual or Transgender relates to a person whose sense of personal identity and gender does not correspond with their birth sex; for example, a pre-operative male to female transsexual.

[For the purposes of LGBT or GLBT in this text 'Homosexuality' will be used to describe forms of sexuality other than heterosexual.]

****

HOMOSEXUALITY HAS STILL some way to go for total social acceptance, though now legalised since the passage of the Marriage (Same Sex Couples) Act 2013, England and Wales. Legislation to allow same sex marriage in Scotland was passed by the Scottish Parliament in February 2014. Gay is anal intercourse, also called *rectal intercourse*. It is common practise among males (Masters and Johnson). Some quote the Bible in their logical morality (so-called) that the anus was designed to reject rather than to receive; though one partner penetrates the other and in their love and intimacy they both arrive. Many a woman when she first encountered a gay man found it to be a great let down for women. Had she considered him less handsome she might have taken a different view...perhaps. Others never condemned anyone, male or female, for being 'different' in their sexual preferences.

Homosexuality goes back since the beginning of time. In ancient Rome homosexuality often differed markedly from the contemporary West. The primary dichotomy of ancient Roman sexuality was active/dominant/masculine and passive/submissive/-feminine. The Roman society was patriarchal, and the freeborn male citizen possessed political liberty (*libertas*) and the right to rule himself and his household (*familia*). Virtue (*virtus*) was seen as an active quality through which a man (*vir*) defined himself. The conquest mentality and "cult of virility" shaped same-sex relations. Roman men were free to enjoy sex with other males without a perceived loss of masculinity or social status, as long as they took the dominant or penetrative role. In other words, he was the *performer* on a *passive* being. Hence the acceptable male counterparts were slaves, prostitutes, and entertainers, whole lifestyle placed them in the nebulous social realm of *infamia*, excluded from the normal protections accorded a citizen even if they were technically free. Although Roman men in general seem to have preferred youths between the ages of 12 and 20 as sexual partners, freeborn male minors were strictly off limits, and professional prostitutes and entertainers were generally considerably older (see Williams, *Roman Homosexuality*, passim; Elizabeth Manwell...Bibliography).

Jesus said nothing on the subject of homosexuality though he lived in the era of the Roman Empire. Many have argued that he did not have to make statements as he was an observant Jew who would have regarded homosexuality as a sin. But this is an assumption and assumptions only make a fool out of you and I. The only people Jesus protested against were the self-righteous and the hypocritical on sin, sins we are all guilty of from time to time. Nonetheless, we have very clear statements from Jesus on how we are to treat others:

Matthew 7:1 - "Judge not lest you be judged".
Matthew 7:3 - "Do not take the mote from your brother's eye until you have removed the beam from your eye."
Matthew 25 - "Inasmuch as you have done it unto one of these the least of my brethren, you have done it unto me". What did Jesus mean here? All were his brothers – sisters included but the Bible was written by men who meant 'man' was human male and female.

All were his brothers – sisters included but the Bible was written by men who meant 'man' was human male and female.

If we follow the teachings of Jesus we will not have the time, energy or heart to condemn our fellow man (Argente, *The Veil*). The question is will we ever know Jesus' views on homosexuality? Is it because Jesus judged not? The morality Jesus taught was to "love your neighbour as yourself." (Mark:12:31), by this love of neighbour he was blind to all else (Matthew 7:3). The righteous who claim to be Christians, to this day, teach morality, a failure to follow the teachings of Jesus:

"Homosexuals need prayers". The preacher is the one who needs prayers because he/she is being judgemental. They should take heed as to how they preach:

In 1 Corinthians 3:10, Jesus said:

> "...like a skilled master builder I laid a foundation, and someone else is building upon it. Let each one take care how he builds on it."

Sadly, our Christian legacy is based upon the paternalism of the founding fathers who spread the message of Jesus according to what politically suited them. They were riddled with issues of power, politics, commerce - God is not a piece of merchandise to be vended, nor is morality. They failed to look upon sex as 'sacred', according to the predilection of the individual. Furthermore, it is by sex we are conceived. The legacy of religion and faith is sadly lacking but that was their concept of the subject within the context of the era and somewhat was spread into the future.

Set aside the draconian Old Testament quotations that relegate sin to things beyond human moral judgment. The New Testament is the era of Jesus and love. And, science has proved that the answer to *all modes* of sexuality is given by Creation and lies in the zygote as to why people are inclined the way they are. A zygote (from Greek "to join") is an eukaryote cell formed by a fertilisation event between two gametes, the first stage of conception (Argente, *Journey of Discovery*). The zygote's genome is a combination of the DNA in each gamete, with all of the genetic information to form an individual:

> "During your life in your mother's uterus, the circulating testosterone may have left a male imprint on your brain cells...during the vital early years, you are better able to respond positively to and copy male models."
>
> Llewellyn-Jones

Androgen is a sex hormone necessary for the development of male genitalia in the foetus. During puberty, androgens are responsible for the development of secondary sexual characteristics, such as the growth of the penis, testes, and pubic hair, the deepening of the voice, and muscular development. *Adrenal androgens* are hormones which are thought to specifically trigger growth of underarm and pubic hair in male and female adolescents (Masters and Johnson).Very rarely this may not work and children are born as female but genetically male. They are insensitive to androgens, male hormones. The Androgen Insensitive Syndrome may be the influencing factor in homosexuality tendencies.

Despite that the dominance of chromosomes gave men masculine traits, there may be the possibility of residual female sexuality in their biological make up, for those who take a female role. Similarly for lesbians who take a male role. Gay is a correlative mode of sexuality (Morris). This shows that homosexual is as natural as heterosexual (Sullivan), but the latter are in the minority and sadly we shall not know the true figures because homosexuals have been obliged to conceal what they are for their self-protection, but we can leave that to Father Time. The written records on the history of homosexuality go back to early BC (Argente, *Difference*). Homosexuality is also found in animal behaviour (Argente, *Caesar and Mapanga Homestead). The Perfumed Garden* briefly describes sex among animals (Nefzawi).

One hundred plus years after the Trials of Oscar Wilde – the love that dare not speak its name - the law's response was the removal of anti-homosexuality legislation which was the blackmailer's charter and disintegrated the power of blackmailers. A good number, mostly men including prominent men, fell under the charter. Homosexuality is found in all societies regardless of rank or culture over the centuries. Had Wilde not been born a hundred years plus earlier he may have escaped the accusing finger of society and the penal law unless his partners were not consenting adults or were minors (Dollimore). Society as a corrupting force encourages the individual to forsake personal conscience for the collective good (Gibran). But then society is a giant chameleon complemented by the law and its changes (Maine) but Father Time, the Master, changes everything including the power of man. [For full discussion, see Argente, *Difference*.]

Between the gays there is true love based on friendship, the stronghold of any relationship; absence of pregnancy, where woman would abort an unwanted pregnancy. To some abstention may be more acceptable than the destruction of human life; the absence of consequent paternal responsibility, unless they wished to adopt children; no contribution to population (the world population is growing at a most alarming rate and one wonders how Mother Earth shall feature in the future); and the ever present component in most human relationships, the quest for equality in sexual union; and in homosexuality there are no gender wars. Furthermore, for the woman who cares for platonic friendship, gay men make wonderful lasting friends, to share intellectual dialogue, a game of sport, or a visit to the theatre sometimes lacking in heterosexual men but so essential to the stimulation of intellect, culture and well-being – at least to some.

Lesbian presents a scenario no less complex because of the attitude of society. Some regard sex between women as less aggressive than gay. This may be due to difference in genitalia. Reasons for the state of lesbian could be: extremity of feminism and aversion to men; the absence of male self-esteem that she owes her orgasm entirely to his sexual skills as a lover, with woman she is less inhibited and she is her own self. Other reasons may be biological, residual masculine traits on the dominance of chromosomes (Morris) found in the zygot (discussed above) where she takes the male role; and the search for equality, which she cannot find in a male partner because of male aggression. In lesbian relationships there is the use of the artificial phallus, any object of size and shape to an erect penis used for stimulation also known as *dildo*. Such devices vary greatly in sophistication, and include battery operated vibrators with warmth and ejaculatory capacity. Some are used with a harness or made double-ended for use in lesbian relationships. Masters and Johnson heralded the use of a see-through plastic phallus for research into what actually happens in the vagina during intercourse (Masters and Johnson).

The University of Newcastle made a breakthrough in creating from a female human embryo for lesbian couples to have their own biological children from the bone marrow of a woman which could be used to fertilise an egg from her partner (BBC Radio 4 22/04/13). Some ask if it is ethical for man to play God the Creator. The point is: Does this harm anyone?

Galatians 5:14: The entire Law is fulfilled in a single decree: "Love your neighbour as yourself."
John 1:17: "For the law was given by Moses, but grace and truth came by Jesus Christ."

In transsexuals there is the tendency by some to dress for the part in the creation of the appropriate schema. Some transsexual men like to dress as women but this is socially unacceptable in public, unlike the position of women who may freely dress as men. Some transsexuals love to adorn themselves in feminine attire and there are more male than female transsexuals. Most of these modes of appropriate sexuality schema are instinctual.

Adults, look back to your childhood, set aside the modesty and you may recall that toddlers, particularly under age 5, played sex together: girls and girls; boys and boys; and boys and girls without instruction or direction from anyone but a fact of nature. Equally masturbation has occupied them subconsciously (Morris), the solitaire child upon the Teddy toy, experience innocent but instinctual sex. It is neither moral turpitude nor abnormality and is as natural in all societies.

Masturbation (Solitaire)

Masturbation (*masturbatus*, classical Latin), is the act of giving one-self manual self-manipulation to stimulate the genitals for sexual pleasure usually to orgasm and is a normal sexual outlet by instinct to exude waste matter through emotion. For those who claim high morality masturbation was seen as an unhealthy indulgence in self-gratification:

"The 'little absolute unto himself' was the masturbating person", so said D H Lawrence. He belonged to the paternalistic era, as Freud who also regarded masturbation as perverse. There is nothing perverse about the mode of sexual preference. Only a perverse mind thinks so. What is important is the person's preference as in the sharing of sexual experience by consenting adults. A fusion of body and soul is a spiritual experience provided no physical harm was done. God would never have created every individual unique if they were to have uniform preferences. Sexual activity, other than genital sex, where the female sucks the male genitalia while he lies indolently, or the male uses his fingers to caress her internally; and vibrators for women, may be regarded as forms of applied masturbation.

In the 19th century masturbation was believed to cause

insanity, blindness and other disorders, probably because people suffering from forms of brain damage were sometimes seen to masturbate in public. Masturbation in public may be a sign of mental illness but masturbation in private is certainly not a cause of it. Methods used in the 19th century in America to discourage childhood masturbation included applying leeches or an electric current to the genitals, castration (male), and clitorectomy (female). There are many of slang terms for the activity including: *crank, flog the tog, jack off, jerk off, toss off, and wank.*

Onanism (self-abuse so-called) comes from the Biblical story of *Onan* (Genesis 38:9-11), who...spilled his seed on the ground so as not to raise offspring...The story is now generally thought to be referring to *coitus interruptus* (Latin: sexual intercourse in which the penis is withdrawn before ejaculation) for various reasons though one is to avoid pregnancy. Onanism is mistakenly still used to refer to masturbation.

Autoerotic asphyxia, also called sexual asphyxia , is a phrase for a form of masturbation, the deliberate reduction of oxygen to the brain to enhance orgasm. It is an extremely dangerous practice, using nooses, gags, etc, carried out by some young men while masturbating. It is estimated that up to 1,000 people die of sexual asphyxia each year in the United States. Recent research suggests that many so-called suicide victims may have been indulging in this practice, and their 'fail-safe' devices failed (McOwen).

Buggery and Bestiality

The *Sexual Offences Act* 1956, s.12 defines buggery as by man with man or woman, and known as sodomy in Scotland and it is a crime when it takes place between two men under the age of 21. Because of the difference in genitalia between male and female the act of buggery had been attributed mostly to men though women also commit buggery (bestiality). In an English criminal court case, a great lady had committed buggery with a baboon and she was conceived by it (R v Bourne 1952).

Bestiality, regarded as sodomy, is human sexual relationship with an animal. It occurs mainly in farming communities, where men and women may attempt intercourse with ponies, calves, sheep, dogs, pigs, etc. Bestiality is against the law and severe penalties can be imposed. Between 1983 and 1993 more than 160 horses were sexually mutilated and stabbed in Britain. British police and animal experts put the blame on fertility cults, rival horse owners and sadists for the attack. One would say the aspect of penetration into an animal is the offence because of lack of consent from the animal, as in the case of sex with a child.

CHAPTER 5

Fantasy

FANTASY IS IN THE PSYCHE and a prerequisite to sex and libido is instinctual, complemented by the external, the anatomy in the fusion of body and mind. Fantasy abounds in its varieties and is unique to each individual turn-on, though two people or a number of persons may share a common sexual fantasy. Adverse factors may blur the psyche and cause the lack of fusion of mind and body, leading to sexual incompatibility. It breeds frustration, the gender war rages followed by a breakdown of *friendship*; sometimes lack of self-restraint by making capital out of the faults of the other and takes away the energy. Some say, there is no such a thing as physical impotence only one that involves a medical condition, rather psychological impotence, a failure or lack of appropriate fantasy and applies to men as women, though there is a general assumption that impotence applies only to man. The difference is one of genitalia more evident in man because of his extroverted genitals. Fantasy as a prerequisite to the act of sex applies both to love and to lust and is the major motivator in sexual activity. Desire with its companion, sexual excitement, happens in a few seconds: a response to a piece of music, scent, smell, or some erotic film or something about the object. The varieties of fantasy are many and the following are only a miniscule.

Group sex *orgy* is the mass licentious revel, the sharing of a common sexual experience simultaneously by men and women, women and women, men and men. The turn-on is the group, competitiveness combined with total lack of modesty in the mingling of covetousness and libido. The *menage a trios* (French) is shared by three, one man two women or two men and one woman together. In these two scenarios competitiveness combine in the absence of modesty, a friendly and playful ambience of hard sex creates the fantasy for sex drive.

The *canine fantasy* reflects a bond between two men (who may claim to be homo-phobic) and one woman. They agree to toss a coin as to who should go first or who would take the talking end, and the element of a friendly competition gives them the sex drive. The canine fantasy may extend to a variety of situations. One is where one of them may have a regular woman and the other would fantasise, while sleeping in a separate room (free audio to the pair's room, such as thin walls) and indulges himself in a solitaire (masturbation). The other is where a father and son share the same woman. The father competing with the son:

"My vital parts still work and I am more experienced than you are." The son attaches his sexual prowess to his youthful physique.

In other instances a man may have two wives, or wife and mistress, or be married to two sisters (common among Orientals). The sharing of one man in one bed at the same time is the turn-on for the trio, an aspect of friendly competition. In societies that practise polyandry, several men married to one woman, and even all brothers may be married to one woman but that is a culture peculiar to their society, for example the Tibetans.

The other is the breasts of a woman. Heterosexaul man remains un-weaned from the mammary, which he transforms from food to a sexual turn-on. In most societies the all time major turn-on in the heterosexuals is a woman's breasts; and in most languages of the world without any apparent connection "mama" is the baby's term for mother instinctively (Argente, *Difference*). Before he became emperor, Nero had sexual relations with his mother Lydia, and incestuous conduct was rife among the Roman emperors and also the Egyptian Pharaohs. The phrase *Oedepus complex* was coined by Sigmund Freud and used in psychoanalysis to refer to the erotic feelings of a son for his mother, at any age; and a sense of competitiveness towards the father. It derives from the Greek legend of *Oedipus,* a Theban hero, who was foretold he would kill his father for his mother's hand in marriage. He left his adoptive parents, killed his natural father unwittingly and married, again unwittingly, his real mother. When the truth was revealed to him he blinded himself. In modern times sexual therapy or counselling would be made available for such a condition.

The dividing line is very fine between the Mother and Lover figures in the carnal desire of man. According to one writer (Williams), Leonardo Da Vinci's portrayal in the face of the Mona Lisa, La Gioconda, captures the aesthetic beauty and division of the mother and playful sex partner at one and the same time. The obsession of some men with 'suck' may be a condition pertaining to the lack of division of mother and sexual partner; as in indolence the applied masturbation by woman's toil for him to 'arrive' in the failure to rise to the occasion for mutual enjoyment. Some men will say anything to woman to have his way with her:

"Semen swallowed is the best nutrition a woman can take".

According to a good number of medical doctors, semen is expired material and has no nutritional value whatsoever, save where it produces an embryoblast. Yet, to the married man only penetrative sex had been regarded as an infidelity (Argente, Difference).

Oral sex, also known as 'coitus foreplay' is the stimulation of genitals by mouth or tongue. Stimulation of the female genitals is called *cunnilingus* (slang *multi-diving*), from Latin *cunnus* vulva + *lingere* 'lick'. Stimulation of the male genitals is called *fellatio* (slang: blow job), from Latin *fellare* 'suck'. Oral sex is practised quite commonly as foreplay to increase arousal or to bring the partner to orgasm. However, a few states in the USA still regard oral-genital sex as a form of sodomy and therefore illegal. Oral sex is also known as 'non-coital sex' which does not involve the penetration of the penis into the vagina (McOwen).

Another form of fantasy was creation of the Bunny organisation operated in London under the entrepreneurs of London and Atlanta City, USA, the ultimate fantasy medium, the abstract aspect of sex. It was the sex object by choice, featured in the *Playboy Magazine*; a somewhat mimicry of the Oriental Geisha, Japanese, the perfect hostess, though sex with the Bunny was no deal. Hugh Hefner founded the sexually explicit men's lifestyle including the magazine in 1953, (1926-died 28/09/17, aged 91, at his home, the Playboy Mansion in Holmby Hills, Los Angeles - Argente, *Difference*).

Fantasy in a different scenario was a man staying in hotels where he asked a chamber maid to take a brush and dust pan and while bending she would brush away dust from the surface of a carpet.

"Faster! Faster!" He would implore her, the faster she went with the brush the higher his libido by which he arrived - nothing to do with contact or the touch of another human being. That was his 'turn-on' for which he paid the chamber maid (Fabian).

Other scenarios include the man asking the woman to make animal sounds: whistle like a bird, hoot like an owl, growl like a dog, and numerous others. So the sex therapist says:

"What does it matter, I tell them, make him happy!"
And, why not? Everything is permissible between consenting adults. However, when the sex therapist was questioned:

"What did women ask from their men to improve their enjoyment of shared sex?"
The answer was that most men abhorred such questions from their women because they regarded them as perverse. Man would prefer to look elsewhere for what he would, by his perception, consider in his woman as perverse, as Urizen tending with jealousy the rose tree, symbol of love, in the garden of experience (Gardner).

Compatibility though may sometimes be a fleeting value but the bedrock of a successful sexual relationship between two people, the absence of which can be a common basis of marital strife from which usually stems adultery; mental and physical cruelty; and friction generally. This is apparent in the high rate of divorce since the sixties particularly by the woman who rebutted the absolute subjugation by man.

Cultural difference can block out the prerequisite fantasy and incompatibility sets in. A certain divorce case in a colonial African setting, the presiding English magistrate asked through a local language interpreter:

"Madam, why have you left your husband?"

"I am tired of a circumcised penis." She replied.
The interpreter was faced with a terrible dilemma and remained silent for a long time. When the magistrate persisted in his question, the interpreter replied:

"She said, they were incompatible, Sir."

Good sex can be an expression of love and trust though making love to his lover the man may be fantasising about Bridget Bardot or Pamela Anderson; while she is fantasising about Judge John Deed or Jerry Rawlings. Other forms of sexual fantasy include telling dirty sex jokes, watching pornographic films and magazines, reading sex books and visually undressing young women, or vaunting on their past sexual experiences to impress, they think, the women around them (Lawrence).

The indiscretions of high profile figures became 'delicious gossip' highlighted by the media (*glasnost* taken too far) since the rise of *perestroika* in the political movement for reformation within the Communist Party of the Soviet Union (1980-1991) associated with the end of the Cold War. This was expressed in *glasnost*, meaning "openness" policy reform of Mikhail Gorbachev. Also men and women who are past middle age and have no sexual partners indulge in the 'delicious gossip', a form of *sexual fantasy*, the closest they can get to having sex. Nonetheless, perestroika and glasnost enriched the English Dictionary.

The perfection, the ideal, of sexual love rests at a *level* which combines two fragments: the abstract in the sphere of the *soul*; and the solidity, the body, connected by emotion, which also belongs to the sphere of libido. The predilection and intention of the mind commands and reflects in the body. The abstract is the first and essential fragment of the combination, and it embodies the values with which the lovers regard each other. The key, as in all human affinity, is kindness in selflessness. The acceptance of efforts made to please the loved one, is reciprocation and felicity in refinement. In short, *grace.* Force of sexual preference is the myth of love. The level is the *equality* of the lovers, whether espoused or otherwise who set aside the constraints of society and the procreation objective and focus on their union. True love is *blind* to and accepts all *differences.* The language of love is mute but decorum in conduct. Since sexual love is a bodily function the attainment of the ideal depends on the purity of the first fragment, the abstract, and the simplicity of the method applied to accommodate the body in its ability to complement the abstract. For the youthful and physically able agility is natural though the less youthful may also attain the ultimate objective in *tantric* sex, an ancient Hindu practise that has been going on for over 5,000 years, and means "the weaving and expansion of energy". The gentleness of touch is the splendour and loveliness of human contact. There are also other qualities which *command* sexual love.

Psychological factors, such as trust and euphoria, create sex drive, which trigger the fusion of hormones by the brain. Contempt, non-constructive criticism, and arguments intensify stress levels, the immune system becomes vulnerable and hormone fusion fails, to the triumph of distress. For some, the commands come naturally, aspiring to the ideal. The bunglers are the disillusioned, the product of absence of acceptance of differences. In true sexual love one receives as much as one gives, a two-way street. The lover who is inhibited by contempt receives nought for he or she is unable to give. The object of the ideal is mutual *orgasm*. Though not all sexual love guarantees orgasm all the time.

The Hite report (1989) describes the absence of give and take, essential to sexual compatibility, a trilogy of 4,500 women aged from fourteen to seventy-eight based on a research in an eloquent testimony of the disturbingly unsatisfying nature of their emotional relationships, out of which only thirty per cent of women achieved orgasm in sexual intercourse. Among other things, the Report asks the question as to whether men love women or simply need them. Man is depicted as more of an aggressor than a lover (Gray). He wants to be the initiator or lest he may accuse her:
"I have never been raped by a woman before".

Some men generally see the female orgasm to mean the measure of male skill as a lover. Such shortcomings may be attributed to social conditioning. Maleness combines the factors of the subject, activity and possession of the male member; and the female takes over those of the object and passivity (Freud).

The Masters and Johnson Studies inferred that the young were sexually active and the non-young were sexually inert; and that as most women grew older they were less fantasising about sex. While the mode of sexual conduct is largely influenced by one's culture sexual response is not the same in any two individuals; each is unique but there are three in each individual: what the person thinks s/he is (egoistic fantasy), what others think s/he is (speculation) and what s/he really is (reality). Response may also stem from chromosomal influence as apparent in the modes of individual sexual preferences and depends on the degree of libido, for men as for women, and sensual sex reveals that penetration and orgasm are not essential to joyful and satisfying sex (Vatsyayana). Sex and love are two distinct separate realities, a distinction much emphasised in Western literature.

Sex is very much a private matter and no one goes on the town square to perform a sexual act. Therefore, sexual preferences done between consenting adults and causes no harm to no one is acceptable or ought to be acceptable; and only thinking would make them seem perverse. Despite restrictions imposed by social and cultural differences or systems of government over the centuries varying from country to country individuals have defied prescriptions and transcended barriers to mate. The mechanics of procreation are blind to differences of any kind and are primordial to the perpetuation of the human species as are other organisms that share Planet Earth. However, to procreate is not always the object when two persons are attracted to each other as apparent in homosexuality which produces no offspring.

One would not expect that the infidelity on the part of either of a pair to a union could be a 'turn on' for some but strange or unbelievable as it may seem, human nature is a complex and an unfathomable phenomenon. While others exhibit jealousy in varying degrees as the following poem symbolises extramarital incident of William Blake's candour to the unrest of Catherine Blake (c.1792):

> The 'rose tree', the symbol of love under Urizen,
> Is always tended with jealousy in the garden of
> Experience...and "here is taken to represent
> Catherine Blake."
> - Gardner, *Literature in Perspective.*

CHAPTER 6

Men and Women

The poor rhinoceros is threatened with extinction for its supposedly aphrodisiac horn. The machismo heterosexual male attitude is appropriately described in crude but truthful language:

> "All the vulgar linguistic emphasis is placed upon the *poking* element; *fucking, screwing, rooting, shagging* are all acts performed upon the passive female: the names for the penis are all *tool* names."
>
> -   Greer, *The Female Eunuch* 1991, Page 47

The above projects the male organ as an instrument of offence. However true this is, not all men direct their organ to offend. Many-a-woman owes her sexual bliss to the well-played organ of the gentle man, to whom we may offer our congratulations for the absence in his intellect of phallocentrism. The word 'Phallocentrism' was used by Ernest Jones (c. 1927) to focus his disagreement with Freud's theory of female sexual identity as being marked by the lack of the phallus (Dollimore). However, it is also true that the thoughts of the heterosexual male in the era of *The Female Eunuch* carried in his mind the three F's towards women: "Find them, fuck them, and forget them." This had been (and still is in 'some' men) prevalent in all societies throughout the world over the centuries from the empires of Romans, Ghengis Khan through to his grand son Kubla Khan, the Bantu across the African continent, to Western European, all licentiously scattered seed in their wake by the three F's. According to one writer the penis is summed up as: "You can show a gun that shoots death, but not a penis, that shoots life. What is the location of the immortal soul of man? The answer is in the testicles where he manufactures his sperm that carry his only hope of immortality" (Morris).

Biblically, when the prostitute woman was being stoned Jesus said:
"Let the one without sin among you cast the first stone" - John 8:7. That was the gentle Jesus in his reproach to the men who had sex with her (they may have been among those who were stoning her). From the Biblical days (possibly even before) man's phalloscentrism was condoned by society, a belief in the superiority of the male sex but Jesus had a way to protect *all* in the prevailing context of that era. To the passive female we may add child sex abuse and animal as both lack consent. Sex with a prostitute, child, or animal are all forms of unshared sex denoting the power of the performer over the object. The prostitute is a consenting party and there is an element of monetary consideration. Sex is not only something shared by two people who are attracted to each other but prostitution is another aspect of sex. The business or practice of engaging in sexual activity in exchange for payment either as money, goods, services, or some other benefit agreed upon by the transacting parties, or a person, in particular a woman, who engages in sexual activity for payment; sometimes described as commercial sex or hooking. A courtesan is a prostitute with wealthy or upper-class clients. Originally a courtesan was a courtier who attended the court of a monarch or other powerful person. In feudal society, the court was the centre of government as well as the residence of the monarch where social and political life were often completely mixed together.

Most societies have historically been more critical of women's promiscuity than of heterosexual men in the belief that man has 10-20 times more testosterone and larger hypothalamus than woman to the chagrin of woman prior to the 1960s (Argente, *Difference*). The crescendo in female promiscuity and showering without raincoats may be evident in pregnancies that usually hit the unmarried. Though there are infidelities among the espoused where a wife's pregnancy is protected in her 'married' status.

The nature of the relationship between man and woman is one that has not escaped evolution in contemporary society. By overt partnership marriage has increasingly given way to the former though marriage remains the bastion of social structure in most societies. The consequences of the marginalisation of marriage is an acceleration of gender wars as woman increasingly rebutted what she considered to be male shackles (Baker, Grey, Lyndon). Dialogue may not confine itself to sexual love, even though the union is an important one, important in the sense that the union, whether espoused or not does not exist in isolation from other aspirations. Respective affinities may be affected favourably or adversely by the nature of the union.

"Twenty-three year old" is the heterosexual geriatric's often-quoted slogan of the woman he fantasises about. In youth the female weapon is the Venus. Legs, legs, all kinds of legs, but what is between them is the object of his fantasy (*Scent of A Woman* movie, starring Al Pacino). As a geriatric he demands for her talking end instead, however – she does all the work, the gift of lechery but when demanded it becomes a chore (Comfort). For the non-Western man to ask for the talking end would be a taboo for such would be an admission to the waning of youth. As the agility of youth abandons the body, man and woman become less enduring in physical prowess. As man grows older ejaculation may take longer to achieve, a bonus for the lovers to take their time –

"Grow old along with me, the best is yet to be"
- Robert Browning

****

To her disbelief he would launder her lingerie.
  "But why?", she would ask.
  "I love what they cover" he would reply.

In the lingerie department he would sit patiently but with obvious delectation while she is choosing her predilections. He would have the pleasure of paying for them and Mammon would never escape his lips to utter its cymbalic sound. He would compose exquisite poetry and write love lyrics and music (if his talent leans that way). He would take her to dinner by candlelight, with red roses and champagne, to dances too. He may be a man's man but he would not dream of spoiling his moments with her by inviting his male friend to accompany them. This is the man to be congratulated. After all, life is but a fleeting melody.

"Men and women are created equal regardless of
their dates of birth and may thereby stimulate a
broader intercourse between the generations."
- Vizinczey

The Adonis may fit in the above picture. He is the splendour of youth (Argente, *Essays and Poetry, The Dreaming Spires of Oxford*). Sometimes called a boy and defined as "A male person who is no longer a child but not yet a man" (Greer). In *The Boy* women are implored to reclaim through his beauty what was reasonably rejected in *The Female Eunuch*. He compensates the older woman against the ravages of time with his boy's physique in endurance so essential to genital sex. But sex with a boy is a form of *irresponsible* sex, though Adonis has passed the 'boy' stage.

The fleeting of youth affects both man and woman. In non-Western societies man and woman each has a personal duty independently of the other and privately to sort out any physical problems that may impair their sexual compatibility by the passing of youth. They tackle such natural problems head on by the use of ancient knowledge of herbs and roots, passed down from generation to generation. Herbs are used to rectify the condition; for women not taken orally and men may chew or drink herbs soaked in water with effects as those produced by Viagra in the Western world. To the body externally applied is the youthful substance from branches of the trunk of *a* tree as aids to youthfulness in activity and in appearance during longevity (Argente, *Enduring Fountain – Health and Wellbeing*). There are varieties of them and all in their natural form. Also warnings about sexual health, and recipes to remedy sexual maladies (Nefzawi).

The ravages of time had not fully marred the beauty of an octogenarian travelling by air and pushed in a wheelchair by an Adonis at change of planes. She was so overcome by his kindness that she said to him:

"de um beijo" ("take a kiss", she was Portuguese speaking in her language).

Had she made that offer 40 years ago he may have been thrilled but alas, he was not yet born then! Such is the irony of life...

Man has been sexually initiated as early as fourteen or less (doubtful by an octogenarian!) at the behest of a guardian. The older woman may find sexual satisfaction in the beauty of the Adonis as some would in a lesbian relationship because of the absence of man's dominance in self-expression to the equality of lovers. To dwell upon the fleeting of youth is a reflection of the parting of geriatrics whose love could not endure the ego and the quest for the prowess of youth. They missed the many splendoured thing as a common bond by the failure to resort to the satisfying pleasures of *tantric* sex.

****

Amrita goes on to explain to Colin the vulnerable position of children who suffer most where the 'friendship' of parents breaks down. Though some parents are more considerate and try to keep some civility for the sake of the children.

Progeny

Society's natural protective instincts of the young suppress early sex education in the Western world (*Children's Act* 1989 *inter alia*). The knowledge in tender years of the beauty of the male and female anatomy and the marvellous mechanics of human conception would carry no belated damaging effects of sexual ignorance. In most non-Western societies the problem of sexuality and sex for male and female adolescents is tackled head on and settled at the outset immediately upon the attainment of puberty. Among African societies youths and maidens receive instruction in the duties of the husband and of the wife respectively, by the 'initiation ceremony'.

The most important aspect of the ceremony is sexuality and the sexual aptitude instruction, which includes a basic form of birth control, the clear coast as the first seven days after a menstrual period. On her first menstrual period the girl is nubile in the natural sense. The sperm of every boy who has reached puberty (Latin: puber = adult) has reproductive value and as such he is a man in the natural sense and both are functionally capable of procreation. Compare the

Western with the non-Western in the Bantu origin (African) and Taoist (Oriental) philosophies on sex and sexuality which favours early sex education as a way of life and generally accepted in those societies (Argente, *Blantyre and Yawo Women*).

In Western societies the individual's perception of the concept of Eros is conditioned from early childhood by law and society; enforced by parents and other educators and seeks to divert the individual from natural instincts and much is left to the state (Freud). The so-called "nanny state" in Britain picks up the pieces wherever parents fail their children and where protective instincts of the young by parents and state suppress early sex education as evidenced by numerous literature and debate on the subject. Some parents are uneasy at the disturbing possibility of raising incestuous thoughts in their children's minds. They withdraw and leave the children befuddled in adolescence. In others sensuality between themselves and their children may be so intense that only the age-old social control prevents the rise of incest (Llewlywn-Jones).

Maurice Chevalier in *Gigi* sings: "Thank Heaven for little girls, for they grow up in the most delightful way". So too, little boys grow up in the most pleasing way. The older heterosexual man, nonetheless, may need the perseverance of some woman, be she a wife, lover, prostitute or a passing acquaintance, to "get him going". Sight of the regular lover alone fails to invoke response. Hence, the blame is directed at woman for man's own inadequacies of sexual prowess. One may assess a man's age with accuracy, however youthful he may look, by his obsession and delight when he sees a younger woman. The Western woman had by the suffragette successfully conquered her second-class role to man in the vote, and the glass ceiling phase in employment as she has the third phase, by sexual revolution. It would seem to be her lot to change in order to hold a man who is too indolent to shift from the *status quo*.

The wife and mother tries to keep it going. What she says somehow comes out wrong. The husband and father's hard look in his eyes tells it all *(Ferguson v Carnochan).* Whatever there was between them has evaporated *(Stevens v Stevens, 1979).* The child does not understand the meaning of the words they exchange in bewildering loud voices and not know what it is all about. The velocity with which the parents do the last minute things before the door slams forever, coupled with the mothers tears and seeing adult tears pains the child; wondering whether he or she has done something wrong, for the world is topsy-turvy. The child wants to do something to show affection but has no idea how (Stone, Stopes). The situation is similar to that of the moment of birth: helpless, handicapped, no limb for touch, no speech to express the feelings (Argente, *Journey of Discovery).*

Kindness and selflessness may exude from parent to infant, who will assimilate values from the adult. No mind is too tender to respond and indelibly impressed upon it the incidents of kindness and selflessness of a parent, grandparent or other caring adult (Ondaatje). The *ideal* will give stability, security, and confidence to the infant, the meridian aspiring to self-*ideal*. Most children know their mothers though they do not know their fathers, in a good number the 'hit and run' syndrome.

Though sentience, the capacity to see, perceive, or experience subjectively gives the human being power of perception at conception and is the essence of our being, awareness and the state of consciousness. Awareness and consciousness is a combined functional and inextricable whole, the ever intrinsically present *self* or ego. From the zygote stage we are all awareness hence the spermatozoa's instinctual velocity to out-race fellow candidates to the fertilisation point. At birth awareness combines the other part of our perception, which is a two dimensional aspect: perception of the natural and classification of the cultural worlds. The first is one's perception of surroundings: the earth, the sky, light of day, dark of night, atmosphere, space, surface of the ground, trees, and so on. And, the second is classification of the arrangement of things into classes according to their common characteristics in the attempt to discover order in our daily lives (Durkheim and Mauss).

A case in point, is the experience of a certain woman: During the Second World War at the age of two years, she, her brother, and mother, were imprisoned by the Japanese in Indonesia (her father was imprisoned in the men's prison). The prison consisted of one large room with mattresses laid along the floor but bare of any furnishings. There were some fifty women and children, each sharing a mattress with her children. The only time they left their mattresses was to go to the toilet next door; thus, they existed for three years till they were liberated by the Allies at the end of the war. When they stepped outside, in her own words she said:

"The intensity and vividness of the numerous colours of the light of day were too much for my eyes." This could be compared to a blind person upon the gift of sight after surgery.

The life of an individual consists of confinement in a specific cell in distinct stages. From the moment of conception the zygote is incubated in the mother's womb for nine months, oblivious to and unaware of external surroundings and travels through a route of development to reach the second stage of confinement. From the moment of birth the individual is coopt in another cell, a fragile, transparent cell through life. The picture of the world through the transparency of the cell is the individual's own image of the world as conditioned to see it, covering a whole host of things including relationships with other people, amid which is also that of sexuality, man and woman via Eros. The second aspect of classification is the cultural or socialisation of the individual:

"The human mind lacks the innate capacity to construct complex systems of classification, such as every society possesses and the model for the arrangement of ideas is society itself."

Durkheim and Mauss.

There are some children who break through the social conditioning barrier. Greg Smith, was a child with a great passion and incredible capacity for learning before he could walk; and he was in higher education before age ten seeking to qualify in medicine and politics. Greg believed that peace starts with children (Winfrey). Social
conditioning is a phenomenon set over many centuries. Therefore, we are ignorant of any possible alternatives as it starts from the conditioning of the infant mind and the model for arrangement of ideas is society itself (Durkheim and Mauss). From the moment of birth the infant's mind will mimic and absorb what society has conditioned and the mind cannot dispense what has not first been absorbed (Argente, *Journey of Discovery*).

"During certain hours, at certain years in our lives, we see ourselves as remnants from the earlier generations that were destroyed...I think all of our lives have been terribly shaped by what went on before us"

(Ondaatje).

Childhood experiences have profound consequences in later life. Children are vulnerable because of their need for a sense of trust. The effects of psychological damage to the male child abused by woman are as lasting as those of the female child who has been sexually abused by man. There are more men than women who sexually abuse children. To the passive female we may add child and bestiality, in the latter two absence of consent. Sex with a child, or animal are forms of unshared sex denoting the power of the performer over the object.

There are more men than women who abuse their daughters. Where the father sexually abuses their daughter the majority of mothers invariably turn a blind eye; or the mother and daughter will become rivals over him. Where the mother sexually abuses their son the husband is likely to be violent to the wife or would even kill her. A man married a woman who had a 4-year old daughter. He began to abuse the child sexually soon after they were married and continued to do so till her adulthood and after she married and had children. Both the mother and daughter remained rivals over him till the mother eventually divorced him. Most children who have been sexually abused, male and female, in adult life naturally become promiscuous, because *practical* sex had been impressed upon a tender mind. Some of the female children who have been abused in childhood become nymphomaniac, a condition describing a woman who has an uncontrollable and unusually high sex drive and who rarely achieves physical or emotional satisfaction. Nymphomania is commonly misused in describing women who have numerous sexual partners. Child abuse is covertly done by the least suspected and the child's vulnerability in the circumstances in which they take place.

The adult woman who takes advantage of a vulnerable male child in playful sexual seduction may not be regarded as an offender in the same sense as the male abuser of a child. Her corrupting sexuality has featured less than that of man because her sexual organs are introverted. There are a good number of men who have been abused by women when they were toddlers, in most societies, Western and otherwise - a form of irresponsible sex by the adult. Since society presumes that such abuse is beyond woman, the real figures may not be known. Because the older woman is in a position of power over the boy aggression may not be overruled and many-a-boy has been psychologically damaged by some woman.

CHAPTER 7

THE VISIT ON THE ISLE OF BUTE WAS OVER and Amrita returned to Dundee. She sat at her Edwardian window, sipping her nettle tea and espying through the lace curtains. On this evening a grey Mercedes pulled up and stopped in front of number One Thousand. Katia was seated in the passenger seat and behind the wheel was who Amrita assumed was some wealthy Nigerian (she discovered later that her guess was right). Katia was living up to her belief that "men should pay..." This was the second time she had seen a car drop Katia. The first time the car was a BMW and behind the wheel was a well-dressed African man.

****

Then there was a knock at her door. It was Kathleen. She appeared distressed, she needed to talk to someone as she poured out her anguish as she sat on the floor close to Amrita's feet:

"I have lost the baby and I have lost him."

She had just had her second abortion both at the university hospital and she never knew the father in both instances. She said that she never bothered about the pill - a form of *irresponsible* sex, for she had been courted by three nice lads at the same time. By coincidence each was named John (she certainly had a passion for the Johnnies!).

Abortion may have given her the desired end but she lived in the trauma of loss mingled with guilt. The media and literature generally inform us that teen-age pregnancies in the Western world where Britain topped the bill were rife and that there were numerous botched up abortions outside the legal confines. Woman's liberation over the top. Easy availability of the pill and abortion on demand. Is there any moderation in our world?

An abortion is the termination of pregnancy before the foetus is capable of surviving outside the womb and was a deliberate intention to rectify a state of affairs. In the UK the limit for induced termination is 28 weeks from conception. Abortion can be performed by surgery or drug treatment but is a criminal offence unless allowed by the current Abortion Acts. Spontaneous or non-induced abortion is commonly known as miscarriage. The physical pain and mental anguish was the same in either. By the advance of science gender selection motivated some abortions in favour of boys once the sex of the foetus was known (BBC Radio 4 on "The Missing Girls").

****

Amrita in her observations saw James, a handsome young man one of the students call on Katia. He lived in Anderson House just across the road. On a particular occasion she saw James with a bottle of wine and a red rose knocking at Katia's door but there was no answer. He left the gifts outside of Katia's door:

"Do you know where Katia has gone to?" James asked Amrita.

"The last time I saw her she was going into her room", Amrita replied.

A few minutes after James left Amrita saw Katia open her door and pick up the bottle of wine and the red Rose.

On the following late afternoon espying at her window she saw a police car, a kind of van with dark windows and four policemen entering Anderson House. She was curious. Then she saw them come out, two sets of policemen carrying a body in a zipped black bag. Loaded the bodies in the van and drove away.

Amrita later learned that James had been besotted with Katia but she just led him on. Amrita pondered on how Katia never opened the door to James and yet took in the wine and the red rose after he left. On the afternoon of the following day in the rooms of a Prince of Arabia, slumped on chairs with two empty bottles of Scotch whisky and a couple of empty glasses on a table, James and the Prince were both found dead.

****

AMRITA COMPLETED HER COURSE and Colin had another year to go, having completed his sophomore year. He visited her at her abode and she continued the final part of the *Kama Sutra.*

"Tell me how you like to be embraced – in the glare of the lights or in the dark?"

"I don't mind the lights."

"Good. We can see each other. Love does not care for time or daylight. This is the Kama Sutra's "loving congress". Amrita continues to school Colin.

"What is the The Kama Sutra?" The well-read Colin had missed the literature on tantric sex.

"The Kama Sutra is a standard work on human sexual behaviour in Sanskrit literature, an ancient Indian Hindu book designed to educate on sex." She quoted:

The difference in the ways of working, by which
men are the the actors, and women are the persons
acted upon, is owing to the nature of the male and
female, otherwise the actor would be sometimes the
person acted upon,
and vice versa" (Vatsyayana).

The Chinese and Taoist philosophy is a holistic discipline that
combines the spiritual and physical aspects. Human beings
should not have only material things...without spiritual
sustenance it is difficult to maintain peace of mind (Dalai
Lama). Everything in the universe is in constant state of
change in the interplay of the great forces of the Cosmos in
two symbolic principles of the *egg/Yin* and *sperm/Yang.* This
is from Nefzawi's *The Perfumed Garden* which presents
opinions on what qualities men and women should have to
be attractive; gives advice on sexual technique; and has a
section on the interpretations of dreams. There are instances
where the man mesmerises the woman by certain
aphrodisiac perfumes to get his way with her. The word
aphrodisiac comes from Aphrodite, the Greek goddess of love
(Argente, *Essays and Poetry,* poem 'Aphrodite') who was
reputed to have been able to lure any male. Over 500
aphrodisiacs have been recorded, though none has ever been
proved to have a genuine aphrodisiac effect. Alcoholic drinks,
especially gin, generally increase sexual desire, but decreases
performance.

"For now, follow a tender beginning." Amrita went on.
The concentrated Chi (energy) in the egg and sperm join in
an energetic dance of life and regeneration. The core is the
fundamental belief that life's journey is for the sole reason
continually to store, cultivate and refine Chi so that one is
able constantly to incorporate, transcend and surmount each

life's experience; and in the exquisite union with another to be filled with both bliss and humility. The philosophy advocates Tai Chi (an ancient Chinese discipline of meditative movements practiced as a system of exercises, also known as *tai chi chuan*) for personal inner refinement to achieve internal peace; and generally recommends martial arts, communication, art, gardening, eating and meditation. The ideal is for the couple's commitment to their own development but mutually sustaining an emerged spiritual development as the Chi spring for a satisfying union in profound spiritual awareness.

Shallow, casual or abusive sex is avoided because of the consequent negativity. Sexual arts are at the core of the Taoist philosophy of wholeness emerging from Chi. Nothing is isolated from it and sexual arts become the very embodiment of the truth of life; enhanced by the woman's fulfilment to a point where bliss was ongoing not a momentary state.

She made him promise that he would refrain from 'demanding of her', whoever she may be at the time, for such would make the gift of love a lechery.

****

THE DUNDEE RAILWAY STATION is typical of most railway stations in provincial Britain of post Victorian style, serviceable without any outstanding features. The layout is a confectionery and newspaper kiosk, a refreshments canteen and two benches at the platform. The empty dismal waiting room is most welcome in the winter months. Colin's early arrival at the station meant a long wait before the anticipated appearance of Amrita.

He notices Angus McManus standing at the platform waiting for the Edinburgh train. He is smoking a cigarette.

"Have a puff. It will keep you warm." He offers it to one of his students, a pretty girl unknown to Colin. She is waiting to catch the same train, as are a good number of other students. It is the end of the semester year. Colin, like others had completed their sophomore year.

"Thanks". She takes it from him. Gives it a couple puffs and hands it back to Angus. Their train arrives. They board for Edinburgh and depart.

Colin is still waiting. Despite that Amrita had implored him not to come to the railway station. As Amrita approaches him, the whiff of Damask Rose hits his nostrils, transporting him to their first meeting. Amrita had taken a taxi from Springfield, sped through Perth Road, a last glimpse of the City of Dundee. She knew of no reason to return despite all the beauty and happiness she had experienced there, not to mention its challenges – but what is life without a challenge? At the end of her course life had reflected the true picture of what her existence had become - here today, where would she be tomorrow?

For travel in comfort she had chosen a sleeveless dress of tailored simplicity made from orange silk floral fabric. Her bare arms reveal a lighter shade of *cafe au lait* in contrast to the shade of her heart-shaped face. She wears no make-up as usual, nature's child, seeking to grasp and hold youth in Mother Nature herself. She is opposed to chemical-based substances or taking any tablets unless it was absolutely necessary. Draped on her arm is a lightweight coat of grey gabardine. She had opted to dispatch her luggage ahead of her departure a few days before, to travel light. She is holding her light hand baggage and a sling bag slung over her shoulder. She had somewhat complicated her life by becoming emotionally involved with Colin.

She recalls a few lines from Thomas Hardy's *Return of the Native*:

"...love lives in perpetuity but dies upon touching."
Again, she thinks of that poem:
"There is no reality, only memory is the reality
"We are but a ripple in the stream of memory."

"We can get married and live in springtime forever", Colin continued to plead as soon as they met. He felt like his life had come to a dead end. He could not and did not feel that he could go on. Younger men felt safer courting menopaused women. There was no fear of unwanted pregnancies and they believed that older women were more experienced. Though it never occurred to him that deep down in his psychological recesses his attachment to Amrita was partly a comforting instinct stemming from the early loss of his mother.

"You should marry a nice woman closer to your own age, and have children". Your whole life is before you". She tried to console him. She had entertained the thought of marrying Colin. What was an age gap? This time it would be the other way round. She was a woman of extremes, chuckling at herself. He would complement her waning form as he could do chores for her, she tried to reason with herself. But that was selfish, a loss of the true love plot.

"I have no wish to reproduce myself. I have been so happy with you." Colin went on.
"When time has healed this moment, you shall feel differently". She tried to reason, wiping away the tears with the back of her hand. They had shared a blissful year that had flown so quickly. For him, it was the happiest of his years, and

even for Amrita who had seen ten Springs more than he had. The whistle of the giant centipede from Aberdeen to Paddington gliding through the curvature of the railway line track announced its imminent approach intensifying the diastole and systole of their hearts. Amrita boarded...the figure of Colin on the platform gradually reduced to a dot in the distance, then nothingness...Brighouse, Dundee, all receding into the past as she took off on the Night Sleeper with the Flying Scotsman.

Bibliography
Sexuality
Argente, Rosemary, *Journey of Discovery*, Epilogue, Amazon (2017); *The Veil*, Amazon 2017 chapter 9, Assumed Divine Mandate*; Difference*, chapter 8, Marriage, Sexuality and Gender; *Blantyre and Yawo Women*, Mzuni Publishers, Malawi, chapter 2, Abduction; *Caesar and Mapanga Homestead*, Amazon 2017; *Essays and Poetry*, Dreaming Spires of Oxford, Amazon - 2017.
BC Radio 4, 25/02/06, Mark Tully's *Something Understood*. This is to mortify and martyr the flesh. Desert Fathers who were no longer persecuted for their belief in Christianity in the fourth century practise the discipline of fasting.
Bly, Robert, *Iron John*, this book contains anthropology, mythology, folklore and legends, helpful for altering the *status quo* for men.
Cline, Sally, *Women Celebacy and Passion* (1993), Andre Deutch Ltd.
Goodwin, Aurelie Jones, Ed. *A Woman's Guide to Overcoming Sexual Fear & Pain* (Relate
    Bookshop).
Marcuse, Herbert, *Eros and Civilisation, a Philosophical Inquiry Into Freud's theory of pleasure principle and reality principle*, where sexuality predominates in instinctual structure.

Llewellyn-Jones, Derek, *Everyman* Oxford University Press, 3rd Edition 1991; p.184, drugs and diseases; p.188 strict moralistic up bringing; & p.190 stress & fatigue; see also Ditto *Every Woman* for the aspect of woman, dedicated to his wife and daughter.

McOwen, Lee, *Making Sense of English in Sex* (Chambers English in Use), paperback published by Chambers January 27, 1993.

Morris, Desmond, *The Naked Man*: A Study of the Male Body; Jonathan Cape; 2008.

Nefzawi, Shaykh, *The Perfumed Garden*, translated by Sir Richard Burton, Introduction by Alan Hull Walton, Neville Spearman Ltd

Sexual *Offences Act* 1967, s.1; *Sexual Offences Act* 1956, s.12 Buggery with or without consent with person of any age or sex or with an animal, life imprisonment; *Bourne* (1952) 36 App. Rep.125, Wiseman (1718) Fortes Rep.91, buggery by man with man or woman.

The Holy Bible, Genesis 38:9-11.

The Kinsey Reports: Sexual Behaviour in the Human Male (1948) and *Sexual Behaviour in the Human Female* (1953), written by Alfred Kinsey, Paul Gebhard, Wardell Pomeroy and others, published by Saunders. Kinsey, American Pioneer of Sex Research and founder of the Kinsey Institute for Research in Sex, Gender and Reproduction.

Vatsyayana, Vallanga, *The Complete Kama Sutra of Vitsyayana* (Page 120). The First Unabridged Modern Translation of the Classic Indian Text. Published by Arcturus Publishing (2012), translated by Sir Richard Burton and F Arbuthnot, eds. With preface by W G Archer & Introduction by K M Panikkar, 1963, George Allen & Unwin Ltd, and its companion *Ananga Ranga* and *The Perfumed Garden*, similar to the comprehensive work *Arabian Nights*.

Wikipedia, *Legends of the Coco de mer; and Peristeria elata.*

Homosexuality

Argente, Rosemary, *Difference*, chapter 6, Minorities, Homosexuality; *The Veil,* chapter 7, Ministry of Yeshua, Sermon on the Mount.

Dollimore, Jonathan, *Sexual Dissidence – Augustine to Wilde, Freud to Foucault* (1993), Oxford University Press.

Gibran, Kahlil, *The Prophet*, With an Introduction by Christine Baker, Wordsworth Classic of World Literature, 1996

Sullivan, Andrew, *Virtually Normal – An Argument About Homosexuality* (1996) Picador.

Williams, *Roman Homosexuality*, passim; Elizabeth Manwell, "Gender and Masculinity," in A Companion to Catullus (Blackwell, 2007).

Fantasy

Argente, Rosemary, *Journey of Discovery,* Epilogue, Amazon 2017; *Difference,* chapter 8,
    Sexuality and Gender, Amazon 2017.

Comfort, Dr Alex, *The Joy of Sex,* classic work (1972).

Fabian, Robert, *London After Dark,* 1945. Fabian was a Bobby on the London beat.

Gardner, Stanley, *Literature in Perspective* (1968), Evans Brothers Ltd, London.

Gesselin, Chris & Wilson, Glen, *Sexual Variations* (1980), Faber and Faber Ltd.

Gore, Margaret, *The Penis Book*, Allen & Unwin. A very helpful book for men's sexuality
    and sexual problems. (Relate Bookshop, Herbert Gray College, Little Church Street,
    Rugby, CV21 3AP.)

Hite, Shere, *The Hite Report,* Publisher Pandora (1989).

Hite, Shere, *Women and Love – The New Hite Report – A*

Cultural Revolution in Progress,
   The Penguin Group.
Lawrence, D H, *Pornography and Obscenity*, *In a Selection from Phoenix*, ed A A H Inglis
   Harmondsworth, Penguin 1929.
Masters, William H and Johnson, Virginia E, *Masters & Johnson Report, Human Sexual*
   Response. Toronto; New York: Bantam Books (1966).
Williams, Peter Vaughan, *The Art of Hypnosis*, Boltonia Print 2000,

Sex Wars
Baker, Robin, *Sperm Wars: Infidelity, Sexual Conflict & Other Bedroom Battles* (1977),
   Fourth Estate, Allen & Unwin.
Gray, John, *Men are from Mars and Women are from Venus,* (1992).
Homicide: The Social Reality, Personal protection on dangerous symptoms of conflict where it escalates into domestic violence and enters the criminal area. See A. Wallace, *Research Study No 5,* Bureau of Crime Statistics & Research. NSW Attorney General's Department (1986).

Lyndon, Neil, *No More Sex Wars: The Failures of Feminism.*
Peace, Alan and Barbara, *Why Men Don't Listen and Women Don't Read Maps,* Orion
   Books Ltd. 2001.

Men and Women
Argente, Rosemary, *Essays and Poetry,* Dreaming Spires of Oxford, Amazon 2017.
Collins, Joan, *Looking Good, Feeling Great*, Robson Books, 64 Brewery Road, London N7 9NT.
Greer, Germaine, *The Female Eunuch*, Flamingo, imprint of Harper Collins (1991)page 47; and *The Boy*, Thames &

Hudson Ltd, ISBN 0-500, 23809X, 181A, High Holborn, London, WC1V 7QX.

Hardy, Thomas, *Return of the Native*, Macmillan & Co. Ltd.

Tolstoy, Leo, *Ivan Ilych & Hadji Murad & Other Stories, Walk in the Light While There is Light.*" (1893), translated by Louise and Aylmer Maude, Oxford University Press 1957.

Vizinczey, Stephen, *In Praise of Older Women* (1967), the amorous recollections of András Vajda (1966). Bernie and Rochliff (Barry Books Ltd), Pan Books 1967. Dedicated to older women and addressed to young men. The connection between the two is the proposition. In 2010, the book was reissued as a Penguin Modern Classic.

Progeny

Argente, Rosemary, *Blantyre and Yawo Women*, Mzuni Publishers, Malawi; *Journey of Discovery*, Epilogue, Amazon 2017.

Children's Act 1989. Courts' paramount considerations. *Child Support Act* 1991 followed the Government Report, *Children Come First* (1990).

Durkheim, Emile and Mauss, Marcel, Introduction by Rodney Needham, *Primitive Classification*, Cohen & West Ltd.; Ditto and with Godfrey Lienhardt, *Social Anthropology*.

Ferguson v Carnochan (1898) 2 White 278, Scottish case where a Judge found repugnant a husband's statement that he could verbally abuse his wife in his own home.

Ondaatje, Michael, *Running in The Family*, 1982; Vintage.

Singh, Indibir, *Human Embryology*, first published 1976, MacMillan India Ltd., 8th edition 2014.

Stone, L, *Road to Divorce* (1991) OUP.

Stopes, Dr Marie, *Married Love* and *Wise Parenthood*, (1918) Winfrey, Oprah, programme 13/03/01.

Marriage

Archbishop of Canterbury Report, *Putting Asunder, Simple Concept of Divorce and*

Breakdown of Marriage.
Dewar, John, *Privileged Position of Marriage. Reform for the Grounds of Divorce. The Field of Choice.* Cmd.3123, Gives additional ground of breakdown of marriage but not as the sole ground for divorce.
James Lewis, *Making Contemporary Britain – Women in Britain Since 1945 – Women,*
     Family and the State in Post War Years (1992), Basil Blackwell.
Legal Aid (Matrimonial Proceedings) Regulations 1977.
Legal Aid not available for undefended *divorces.*
Maine, Henry James Sumner, *Ancient Law* supplemented in *Early Law and Custom;* 1861, John Murray Albemarle.
Marriage, Sacred Union or Determinable Contract, K O'Donovan, O*n Family Law Matters* (1993.
Matrimonial Causes (Consolidation) Act 1973. Legal framework for all matrimonial proceedings. *Matrimonial Proceedings & Property Act* 1970. Courts have powers to make financial provisions and property adjustments.
Report on Matrimonial Causes Procedure Committee (HMSO 1985) under the
     Chairmanship of The Hon. Mrs Justice Booth, para 2.8.
Royal Commission on Marriage and Divorce. Cmd.9678, *The Morton Commission.*
     Concept of no fault divorce.
R v Nottingham County Court, ex.p Byers [1985] 1 All ER 735, Per Lately J at p.737 –
     undefended divorce dispensed with the need to Appear in court of either party or their representative.
Serio v Serio (1983) 4 FLR 756. Rebuttable to prove illegitimacy.
Stevens v Stevens [1979] 1 WLR 885. Husband's behaviour was such she could no longer reasonably be expected to live with him.
Strongfellow v Strongfellow [1976] 2 All ER 539. Wife failed

to prove unreasonable behaviour.

Weitzman, L *The Marriage Contract*, L (1981). *Legal Regulators of Marriage, Tradition and change.*

A tragedy set in Dundee, at the time of the rise of the mature student in a European Union university...about the adventures of sophomore, a male virgin, and a mature woman who becomes his mentor on sexuality...their life within the university student community, what was happening around them, and their separation...

This is a good read with a lot of interesting facts on sex (very well referenced) and framed by a decent fictional account of Amrita's experiences. The setting too is well described and evocative of scenic Scotland - Salma Khan.